This Walker book belongs to:

_____

_____

_____

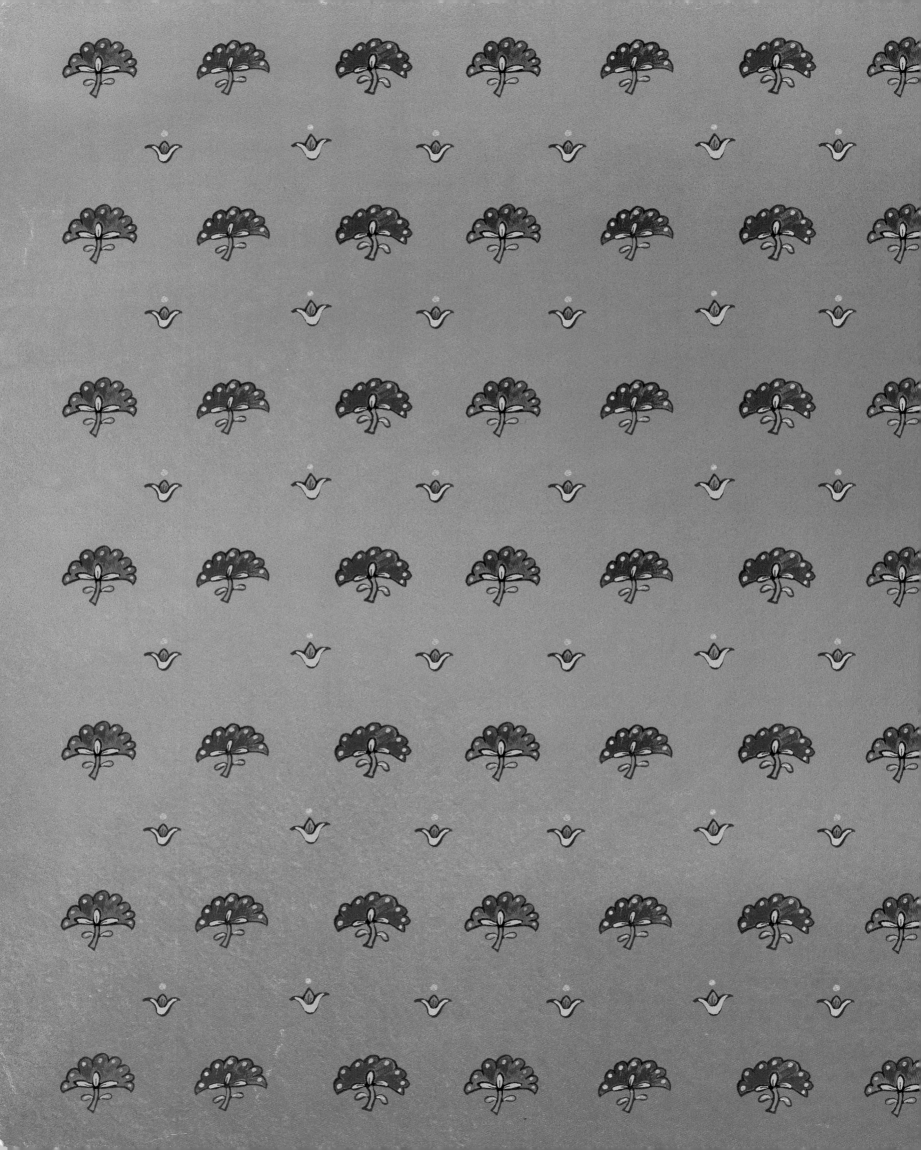

For Esme, a true citizen of the world!

Dear Reader,
This is a picture of my little friend Esme
and her family. Esme was born in China,
but her mum is Welsh and English
and her dad is Indian. Lucky Esme –
she has a toe in four different countries!
This book is to remind Esme of her
Indian family and friends, and to give
you a chance to take a walk through
India with some of its fantastic animals.
Namaste,
Marcia

The Elephant's Friend and Other Tales from Ancient India

Retold and illustrated by

Marcia Williams

WALKER BOOKS
AND SUBSIDIARIES
LONDON · BOSTON · SYDNEY · AUCKLAND

The Elephant's Friend

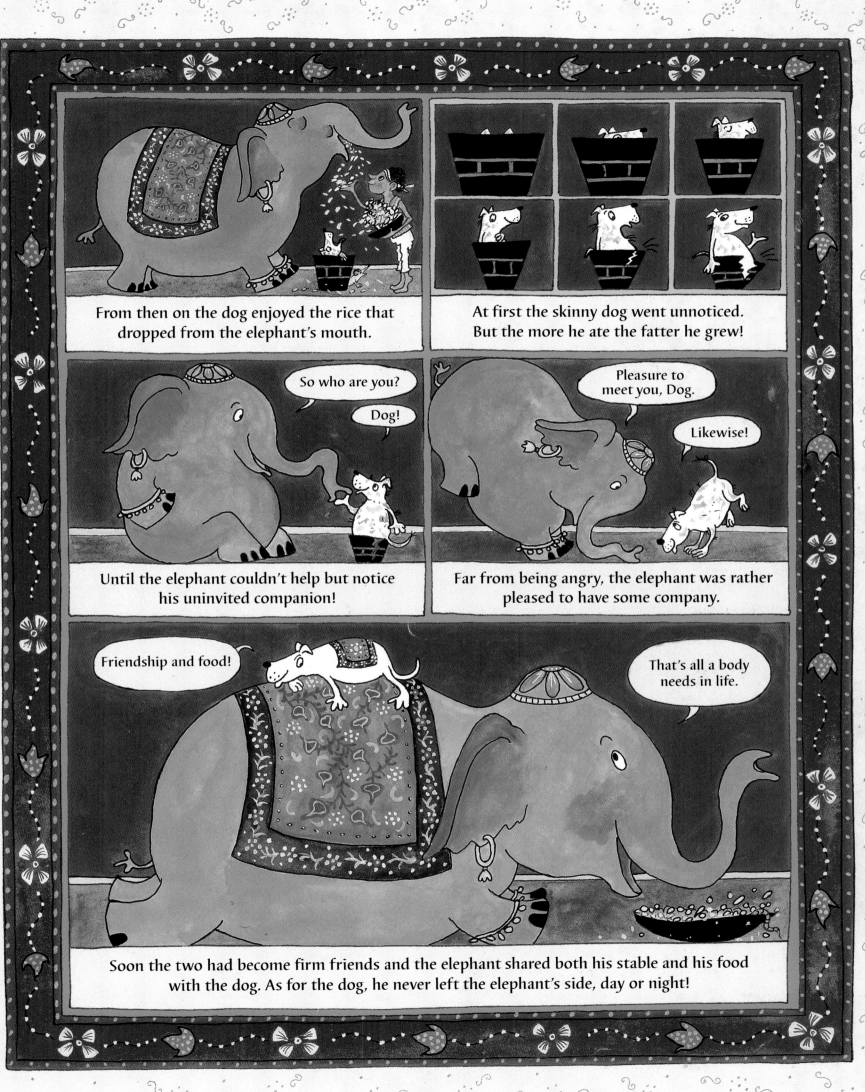

Eventually the king's proclamation reached the village where the dog and the merchant lived. The threat of punishment really scared the merchant, so he chased the dog out of his yard and down the hill! With his tail wagging all the way, the dog ran helter-skelter back to the elephant.

The elephant and the dog danced with delight while the king, his ministers and the elephant's keeper all cheered and clapped. And so the two friends lived contentedly together for the rest of their days and nobody, but nobody, ever tried to part them again!

The Scrawny Old Tiger

All might have been well if some villagers hadn't spotted them. The villagers burst into laughter at the sight of two geese carrying a tortoise. Kambugriva was furious! He opened his mouth wide to admonish the villagers and fell tumbling from the sky.

Poor Kambugriva, he was never, ever heard from again!

The Wise Little Pebet

All her sons soared into the sky except the very youngest, who failed to take off.

He tried and he tried and he tried, but he just couldn't make it.

So Little Pebet was caught in the claws of the hungry cat! He was just about to pop Little Pebet in his mouth, when Mother Pebet suggested he would taste better if his sticky feathers were washed!

So the cat washed Little Pebet.

Then dried him by twirling him round and round on his paw.

On the seventh twirl, Little Pebet managed to get airborne ... but not before he had left a little offering on the cat's paw! The cat watched in horror as his meal flew up, up and away ... and as he watched, he absent-mindedly licked his paw!

The Golden Swan

Once upon a time there was a swan with feathers made of the purest gold.
The swan lived on a fine pond and was rich in both food and friends.

Close by the pond there lived a poor mother with her two daughters.
Their clothes were rags, their food meagre and their luxuries non-existent.

The swan felt sad that they had so little and he had so much.

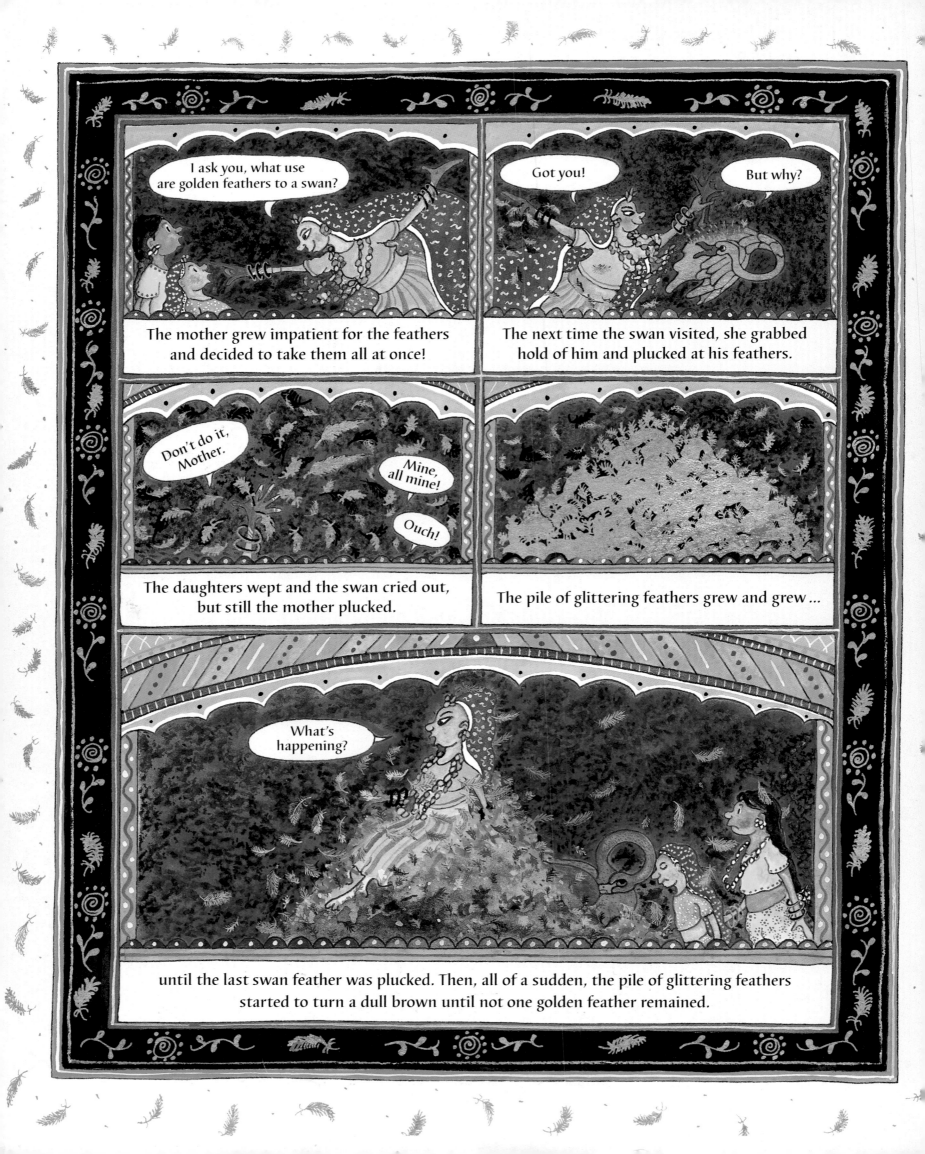

The mother and her daughters gasped in horror, but it was too late. The swan took his leave of the ungrateful woman, who had returned his generosity with such greed. He went with his friends to live in a far distant land, never to return to the little shack again.

The Monkey and the Crocodile

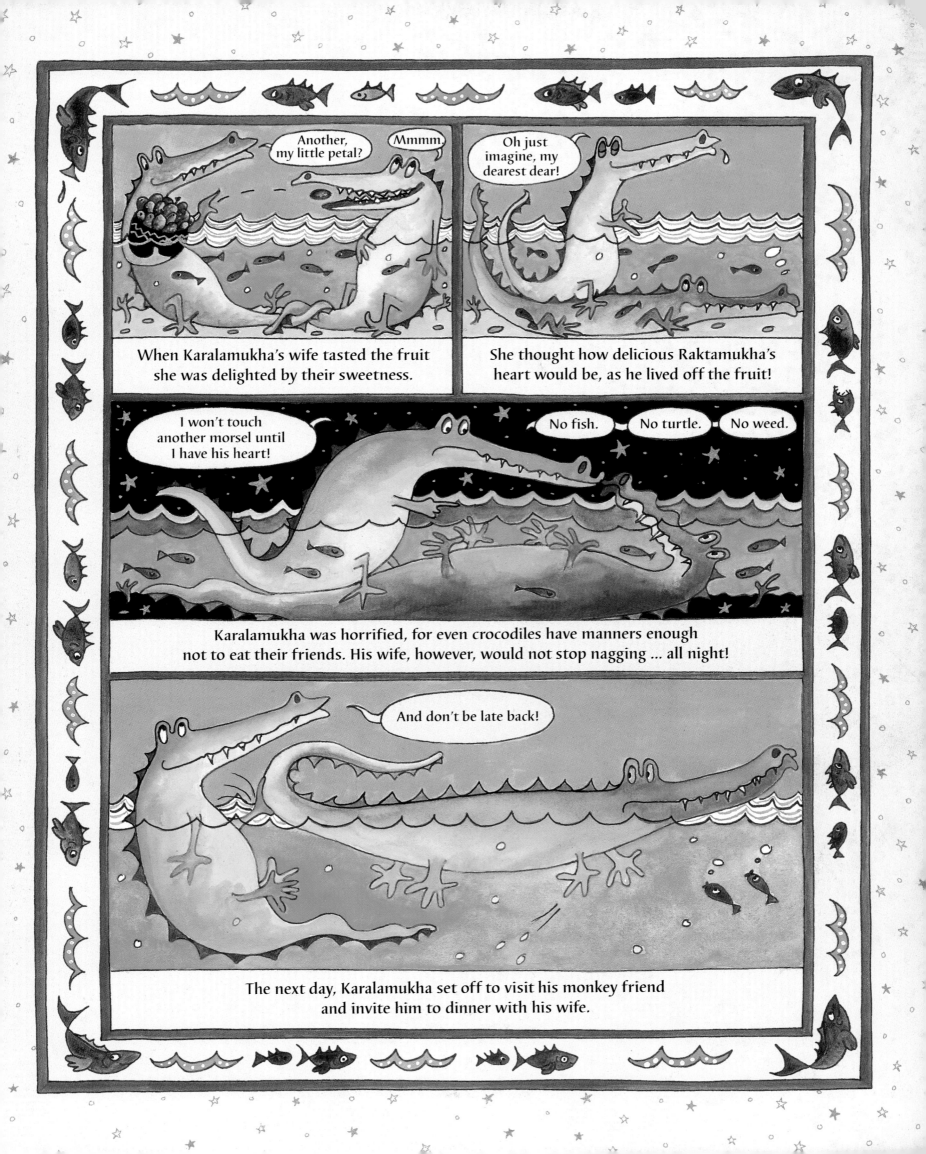

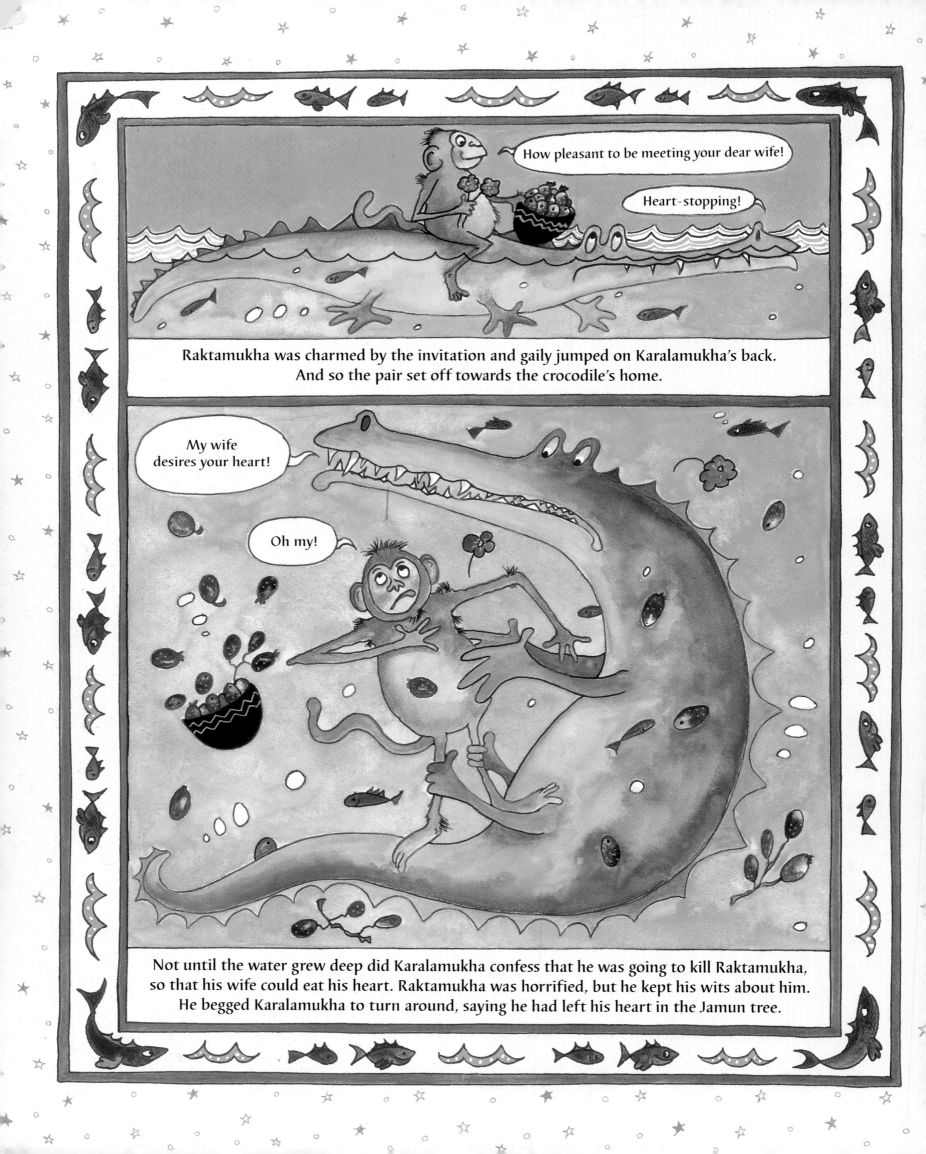

Raktamukha was charmed by the invitation and gaily jumped on Karalamukha's back.
And so the pair set off towards the crocodile's home.

Not until the water grew deep did Karalamukha confess that he was going to kill Raktamukha,
so that his wife could eat his heart. Raktamukha was horrified, but he kept his wits about him.
He begged Karalamukha to turn around, saying he had left his heart in the Jamun tree.

The Tale of the Three Large Fish

However, his two friends preferred to take their chances in the lake,
so the wise fish left on his own.

The very next day the fish that believed in fate was caught in the net
of the fishermen and that was the end of him!

The clever fish was also caught in the net. However, being clever, he pretended to be dead. So the
fishermen cast him back into the lake. There he lived for the rest of his large, clever and rather lonely life!

The Foolish Lion

In the middle of a forest there lived an extremely greedy lion named King Bhasuraka.
King Bhasuraka ate at least six forest creatures a day!
He grew fatter and fatter, but the forest creatures grew fewer and fewer ...

until the animals offered to send one animal a day to King Bhasuraka's den,
to be killed and eaten. As this would save him hunting, Bhasuraka agreed.
But if an animal ever arrived late, Bhasuraka said he would kill all the animals left in the forest!

So every day a forest animal was sent to King Bhasuraka's den, never to return. Bhasuraka found this suited him very well and made him feel extremely kingly.

Now the day came when it was the turn of a wise old rabbit to serve himself up for supper. Old as he was, he was not a bit happy about being eaten. So he hopped very slowly towards Bhasuraka's den, wondering how he might avoid his fate.

By the time Wise Old Rabbit reached the lion's den, Bhasuraka was roaring with impatience. When he saw the skinny old rabbit appear he roared even louder!

Wise Old Rabbit apologized profusely for his lateness and his smallness. He explained that he had set out with five companions but another lion, who also claimed to be king of the forest, had eaten them. When King Bhasuraka heard this he almost exploded and swore to tear the impostor to shreds!

So that was the end of King Bhasuraka!
Wise Old Rabbit gave a little hop of relief and went to tell his friends the good news.

Although he was old and weak, Wise Old Rabbit became the forest hero
for he had shown that wisdom can overcome physical strength.

First published 2012 by Walker Books Ltd
87 Vauxhall Walk, London SE11 5HJ

This edition published 2013

2 4 6 8 10 9 7 5 3 1

This book has been typeset in Barbedor and Ondine
Handlettering by Kate Slater

Printed in China

British Library Cataloguing in Publication Data:
a catalogue record for this book
is available from the British Library

ISBN 978-1-4063-4492-9

www.walker.co.uk
www.marciawilliams.co.uk

Marcia Williams

With her distinctive cartoon-strip style, lively text and brilliant wit, Marcia Williams brings
to life some of the world's all-time favourite stories and some colourful historical characters.
Her hilarious retellings and clever observations will have children
laughing out loud and coming back for more!

ISBN 978-1-4063-3918-5

ISBN 978-1-4063-3832-4

ISBN 978-1-4063-2997-1

ISBN 978-1-4063-2610-9

ISBN 978-1-4063-1944-6

ISBN 978-1-4063-2334-4

ISBN 978-1-4063-2335-1

ISBN 978-1-4063-0563-0

ISBN 978-1-4063-0562-3

ISBN 978-1-4063-1137-2

ISBN 978-1-4063-1866-1

ISBN 978-1-4063-0348-3

ISBN 978-1-4063-0347-6

ISBN 978-1-4063-0171-7

ISBN 978-1-4063-0940-9

ISBN 978-1-4063-1002-3

Available from all good booksellers

www.walker.co.uk